Powell's First Lady of Civil Rights: Rosa

$33.99 / 5.95   PC

Children's   117458

THE FIRST LADY OF CIVIL RIGHTS
ROSA PARKS

By BRUCE BEDNARCHUK

Illustrated by MARCIN PIWOWARSKI

CANTATA LEARNING

MANKATO, MINNESOTA

CANTATA LEARNING

MANKATO, MINNESOTA

Published by Cantata Learning
1710 Roe Crest Drive
North Mankato, MN 56003
www.cantatalearning.com

Copyright © 2015 Cantata Learning

All rights reserved. No part of this publication may be reproduced
in any form without written permission from the publisher.

Library of Congress Control Number: 2014938327
ISBN: 978-1-63290-087-6

The First Lady of Civil Rights: Rosa Parks by Bruce Bednarchuk
Illustrated by Marcin Piwowarski

Book design by Tim Palin Creative
Music produced by Wes Schuck
Audio recorded, mixed, and mastered at Two Fish Studios, Mankato, MN

Printed in the United States of America.

Rosa Parks
(1913–2005)

In 1955, a bus driver told Rosa Parks to give up her seat. She refused and was taken to jail. Many people began to **protest**. The **Supreme Court** ruled that all people should be treated equally. Rosa Parks is known as "The First Lady of **Civil Rights**" for helping to bring about this change.

That famous day in 1955,
on a bus a seat was denied.

She was a different color than her white
friends, whom they didn't bother.

The driver told her to give up her seat,
"Go to the back and stay on your feet!"

This was the law, if you can believe.
Not all Americans were free.

Some would only feel bad and cry,
but Rosa Parks was one to try

and make a point to protest. These rules are just plain silly.
They're not going to fly.

She said she would not give in to fear.

It takes **courage** to stand up for what you believe.

That famous day in 1955,
on a bus a seat was denied.

She was a different color than her white friends, whom they didn't bother.

The driver told her to give up her seat, "Go to the back and stay on your feet!"

This was the law, if you can believe. Not all Americans were free.

The bus driver made a demand,
and someone needed to take a stand.

Rosa knew the rule was not right,
and she stood up for what she believed.

So Rosa Parks became the model
for others to learn and follow.

She gave hope to all who wanted to be free.

That famous day in 1955, on a bus a seat was denied.

She was a different color than her white friends,
whom they didn't bother.

The driver told her to give up her seat,
"Go to the back and stay on your feet!"

This was the law, if you can believe.
Not all Americans were free.

Rosa Parks was arrested, and the laws were then tested.

She had done the unexpected, and it was about time.

There was a protest and then a **boycott**, which means others joined the fight. The law was unjust and unfair.

It was based on **race** and just not right.

Rosa Parks stood up for what she knew was right.

In fact, they called her "The First Lady of Civil Rights."

It took courage, but she knew that others were wrong.

Rosa was able to change the laws just by being strong.

The bus driver made a demand.

Rosa knew the rule was not right,
and someone needed to take a stand,
and Rosa stood up for what she believed.

So Rosa Parks became the model
for others to learn and follow.

She gave hope to all who wanted to be free.

GLOSSARY

boycott—to refuse to buy or use certain goods and services

civil rights—freedoms that every person should have

courage—bravery

protest—to openly disagree with something

race—a group of people with the same ancestors

Supreme Court—the final judge in all cases in the United States of America

First Lady of Civil Rights: Rosa Parks

Bruce Bednarchuk
Pop Rock

Online music access and CDs available at www.cantatalearning.com

ACTIVITY

1. Rosa Parks was a leader. What are the characteristics and behaviors of a leader?

2. What would you do if you were asked to do something that you think is unfair?

3. What changes do you think would make our world a better place?

TO LEARN MORE

Chanko, Pamela. *Rosa Parks: Bus Ride to Freedom*. New York: Scholastic, 2007.

Edison, Erin. *Rosa Parks*. Mankato, MN: Capstone Press, 2013.

McDonough, Yona Zeldis. *Who Was Rosa Parks?* New York: Grosset & Dunlap, 2010.

Schaefer, Lola M. *Rosa Parks*. Mankato, MN: Capstone Press, 2002.